Love the Hurt

Also by Robert Horne and published by Ginninderra Press

The Undergrowth & other stories

Robert Horne

Love the Hurt

Love the Hurt
ISBN 978 1 74027 798 3
Copyright © text Robert Horne 2013
Copyright cover image © deviantART – Fotolia.com

First published 2013
Reprinted 2016

GINNINDERRA PRESS
PO Box 3461 Port Adelaide 5015
www.ginninderrapress.com.au

Contents

Cassie Flies Home ... 7

Fireman ... 14

Flinders Fields ... 20

Killing James Brown ... 28

Love the Hurt ... 37

Pearl Earrings ... 46

Snake ... 57

The Beach ... 66

Cassie Flies Home

The red car sat in her parents' drive and the way was clear behind it, as she knew it simply had to be. It reminded her of a toy soldier or of the British Grenadier that was in her Social Studies book at school when she was eleven years old. Cassie felt certain the car would know exactly what it had to do that morning without it even having to be told. She was quite excited.

Cassie gave the taxi driver twenty dollars and waved away the change. She would not need it where she was going.

An elderly lady with a small white Samoyed dog approached the house along the shady footpath.

Cassie grinned and cried, 'Good morning.'

The woman picked up her little dog and watched, puzzled, as Cassie stepped briskly past; that girl had always been so sullen before.

Cassie walked firmly up the gravel driveway, then slowed as she got to the car, feeling its magic power and respecting it. She paused at the car's front grille and then went slowly all around it, patting the duco admiringly as she did, and back to the grille again. She stroked the bonnet and to her astonishment she thought she saw a headlight wink. She winked back at it and waited; nothing happened but she wasn't surprised – you can't force these things, you know. She crouched and tried to look at the car's brain inside the grille, but couldn't see a thing.

'What are you waiting for?' said the car as plain as day. 'We're all ready to go.'

'Jolly good,' cried Cassie. 'But can I get some things first, to take with me? They might help us get there more easily.'

The car frowned its little grille and Cassie was afraid it was going to be mad with her. 'Hmmm, I don't know.' Then it shrugged its little mudguard. 'Oh, all right, but I wouldn't take all day. We've been waiting for you.'

The car was acting hurt, but Cassie knew she didn't mean it.

'Are there some others coming?'

'Oh, there are lots of us.'

'Goody,' said Cassie, really excited now. This was going to be a wonderful day.

'Off you go, then. Be quick, and don't let anyone know. It has to be a secret.'

Cassie turned to go into the house but one thought was still stopping her. She turned back to the car. 'You're not going to make me normal, are you? Like other girls?'

She saw the car's shoulders slump, as if with disappointment that she could say such a thing.

Its little headlight peeked around at her. 'Do I look normal... myself?' said the car.

Cassie was convinced. 'Sorry,' she sang, and skipped happily around the side of the house.

Across the road was old Mr Worthington, clipping his hedge as you would expect on a Sunday morning. He looked up as Cassie climbed the two steps to the front porch. Cassie smiled and waved a sharp little salute with her right hand raised as high as her shoulder – she didn't sing out good morning, that would have been risky as she could have given away her position to the others inside. Mr Worthington looked blankly back at her.

Cassie closed the front door but left the lock clicked in so she could open it easily if she had to rush out. She stole up the passage in her socks; her tennis shoes were in her hand and she giggled quietly to herself. There were voices in the kitchen. She could hear her mother, who had been sending her messages through the electricity wires, and she could feel that her father was there, silent and gloomy. But the other two were there as well, her sister and that dreadful Eoghan Regan who had been following her around for months. She had been hiding from him for a week and she was happy because none of them were ever going to find her now, after this.

She tiptoed into her room. From the wall she picked the aircraft poster she'd had since she was a little girl, and carefully scratched the Blu-Tack from the corners so there wouldn't be a mark on the face of the print when it was rolled up – what a good girl! She tucked the rolled-up poster under her arm; if that didn't help her to fly, then nothing would. She pulled a shoebox full of old things out of a drawer and found her *Bananas in Pyjamas* tape and slipped that into her bag – brilliant. Lastly she opened a drawer and found her old teddy bear with his perfect, sad face. Now she was ready to go anywhere.

She saw the red car straighten up as she walked back up the drive: it had been slouching very badly. Cassie put the key in the lock for the first time and what a shock as all four door buttons sprang up at once.

'All aboard,' sang Cassie.

She jumped into the driver's seat and started up the car then found reverse gear. She'd forgotten to put the tape in, so with one hand she fished it out of her bag and jiggled it into the player. She pressed a button and the lead-in tape began to move.

'Away we go,' she cried happily and reversed down the drive. But as she did so she looked in her mirror and saw her sister and the dreadful Eoghan; they were blocking her way on the drive.

She put her foot down on the pedal and as she accelerated they scattered like magic, one flat against the wall in fear and the other sprawled on her arse in the bushes. She sped into the street and began to reverse up Golden Elm Way.

But when she looked in her mirror, she thought she saw a car coming down from Unley Road – it looked like an old red Mercedes and she knew who would be driving that car and it would be her uncle and he would be looking for her too. She began to panic: the plan of reversing to the past was not working straight away. She wrenched the car to first gear and sped away down the street to the T-junction at the end. Now the tape began to play. There was a guitar strumming slowly and forcibly. It quickened pace and then some kind of electric organ played a theme over it. This was not *Bananas in Pyjamas*. A single male voice began to sing mournfully.

> When the routine bites hard
> And ambitions are low
> And the resentment rides high
> But emotions won't grow
> Taking different roads
> Then love, love will tear us apart again

'Aarrgh,' she screamed quietly. The tape she'd pulled out of her bag had not had a case around it as the one from her bedroom drawer would have had, and there was no time to change it now. It was *Love Will Tear Us Apart* by Joy Division. She didn't want that any more: it was nasty stuff. Nothing was going to plan but she was sure it would work out soon.

She turned right in a hurry. If she put space between her and the red Mercedes, perhaps everything would be all right.

She turned left, then right, then left again. The car was very noisy, not at all like she'd expected from a brand-new one. And she couldn't get it to go fast enough.

The woman with the dog stopped and stared at her again. The fluffy white Samoyed reminded Cassie of a little polar bear.

She slowed down and waved to the woman. 'Why don't you take him to the fish shop? That's what they like.'

The woman seemed not to understand.

'Bears like fish,' Cassie cried.

'Second gear.' The woman raised her voice over the revving of the car. 'Use your gears.'

Of course, thought Cassie. She remembered now. She put the car into second and put her foot on the accelerator to race away, but it stopped abruptly in the middle of the street and Cassie bumped her forehead on the steering wheel.

'Why don't you help me now?' Cassie shouted in vexation at the steering wheel but the steering wheel said nothing in reply. In the mirror she saw familiar figures hurrying up the street towards her. She would have to do something under pressure now, but she was used to that. She put her left foot on the clutch, started the car again and revved it hard with her right. She slowly eased her foot off the clutch and the car began to move again, jerkily at first, but she was away.

'Yes, yes, yes,' Cassie shouted, triumphant. She was going again and it was better this time. Second gear was brilliant compared to first!

Cassie's little family of pursuers jogged up to where she'd started her take-off and saw the red car disappear around the T-junction at the end of the street.

The woman had picked up the Samoyed again, as if to protect it. The dog licked up at the woman's face and she made no move to stop it.

She turned to them. 'That girl told me to feed fish to my dog,' she said, then turned her head back to the corner round which Cassie had disappeared.

Cassie turned more corners and had lost her way completely but knew that if she kept going long enough she would find Unley Road. Then she would be ready to fly backwards over it and into her past and her happy childhood cottage that she knew was still there.

Each corner could be it, but wasn't. She began to panic again.

The first song had finished but then another one started.

> Confusion in her eyes that says it all
> She's lost control
> And how I'll never know just why or understand,
> She said I've lost control again
> And she screamed out kicking on her side and said,
> I've lost control again

She didn't like that song; it was even nastier than the first one. She wanted to change to *Bananas* but she didn't dare stop and fiddle in her bag now – those crazy people following her might be just around the corner. She had to get away. She turned another corner, knowing that it had to be the one. But no. The sign said Aylesbury Street or something like that – nothing like Unley Road.

The tape player went on and on.

> And she told me all the secrets of her past
> And said I've lost control again.

'No, no,' Cassie yelled out. She started hitting the steering wheel in frustration. Her face was hot and she began to cry. The next street sign said Addison Avenue. She jammed the stick into first gear and headed straight for the sign in her anger. The front left headlight crashed into it and she reversed out, back into the street. That was better – she was showing these stupid signs. She was master of the car now; driving was easy. The next rogue sign she sped up and drove right at but steered away at the last moment and screeched into it, smashing the car broadside just behind the driver's window. The feeling of the metal sign smashing into the car just behind her head was exciting. She felt the impact of shards of glass on the back of the headrest and heard them tinkle as they hit the floor. She accelerated again and scraped along the side of a car parked in the way; she felt the left-hand outside mirror rip away but she was off again.

She passed a street on her left and glanced up it to see what was at the end and there at last was a more important road. She thought she saw a bus rumble by, like some big yellow caterpillar. She blinked twice then braked hard and could smell both burning oil and rubber: it reminded her of the day Mum had left the chip oil on the stove too long. Cassie cried with relief. She could see now that all this driving around had been planned as practice, like perfecting a cross-court backhand. She and the car had started to work together, now it was time to fly.

Cassie edged into the street and began backing up towards Unley Road, trying not to be too excited. This was it. She stopped eighty metres short and placed the car in neutral.

Joy Division were still playing.

Perfect. She would not just dance, she was going to fly. If she could fly this car backwards over Unley Road to her old home in Fullarton, she would turn back time and live in her childhood once again. She checked her bag: *Bananas* were there and so was Teddy – perfect. She picked the aeroplane poster off the floor, folded it over and tucked it down the front of her shirt. Slow Sunday traffic passed up and down Unley Road and on the other side was a golden elm tree full of the fresh growth of spring. Cassie smiled because she'd be going over the top – the first girl ever to fly a car.

'Goodbye,' she said to the world, to herself.

Cassie re-engaged reverse and built up speed. An old man stopped and stared, Cassie waved happily. She built speed, faster, faster, faster, and suddenly the road was there and she was in the middle of traffic. There were sharp, sudden screeching sounds: a car horn honked hard and brakes were so close it made Cassie's eyes open wide with the electricity that surged through her. Up, up, up she felt her heart soaring. Then a crashing thump and another tinkle of glass and she hit the headrest of the driver's seat hard with the back of her head. She could see another car stopped right in the middle of the road. It had swerved so that its back was pointing towards the front gate of the house opposite and the driver was facing towards her. What a funny thing to do. And the look on his face, as if he'd put money in a slot machine and a dolphin had popped out.

Cassie began to laugh. She laughed and laughed and couldn't stop.

There was the smell of burning rubber, and of petrol spilt on the hot road.

Cassie grabbed her bag and quietly closed the door of the car, still laughing at the face of the stranded driver, then walked away to find her childhood.

Fireman

There is a moment in the film *The Graduate* where the Dustin Hoffman character wanders confused through the graduation party his parents are throwing and an old friend of the family takes him aside to give him just one word of advice as he sets out on the road of life. Dustin has been finding little meaning in the gross material existence his family has presented him. This could be the gem, he thinks, that will make it all come together.

'Plastics' is the one word. Get into plastics.

That family friend was right in his way; plastics took off. But it wasn't the kind of advice that Dustin was looking for. By 1967 the world already had plenty of antidotes for that kind of thinking. The voices were there: Kerouac, Dylan, Stones. Some of the right people even winkled out old albums by Leadbelly and Woody Guthrie from second-hand record stores and began exploring another world of injustice and resistance.

I still have the records, and a player with a needle that works. It's an irony that so many of the CDs I bought that cover the same ground became scratched and won't play any more, or stop in the middle of a song, silence darkening the void the music had been meant to cover; the new technology conked out before the one it replaced. Sometimes I put on the old vinyls that just keep going around and around, the odd pop and scratch still in the same place it was twenty years before. A bit like the people who play the records, I suppose.

For some reason, all this stuff came back to me when I bumped into someone I used to know. We haven't been friends for years and there are probably good reasons for that. And some days you might cross the street or go into a shop to avoid the contact. But this time James had seen me first and saluted like we were old friends, which is maybe the way things could be if you stretched them out a lot and crammed them back into a shape that was a social nicety. He suggested having a drink. We were right outside the King's Head Hotel and they have a nice little lounge and it was a Friday afternoon and it was after four and I'd done my marketing, so it hardly seemed an offer I could refuse on reasonable grounds.

James had broken up with Lucy and maybe that explained his eagerness to make friends again. Lucy had always been brittle and winning, her head ticking like an alarm clock. After he met her, new friends began to appear in his world. It might have been something to do with the night we all went back to her place, to the family room at the back of the parents' house. I dimly remember a pool out back with curved sides, like a kidney shape or something like that. But it was winter time and a cold night at that so we were for the inside. Someone fished out the soundtrack of the film *Borsalino* and slipped on the tango scene. I can't remember if I was playing the part of Jean-Paul Belmondo or Alain Delon, but as old pal Colin and I turned for our third run of the room somehow the longneck which had been held in our clasped-together leading hands slipped out and made a bit of a broken-glass-and-foaming-beer type mess on the parquetry.

We didn't see much of them after that.

But now it seemed that James had some time before also bumped into the very same Colin who had once been my tango partner. James had received the latest news on Colin's not very impressive progress through life. A rented flat in some block at Glenelg, doing odd jobs and mowing lawns, all with the clouded eyes of the lifetime dope smoker.

I wasn't that surprised to hear it. If Colin had made it big in something, that would have been the real talking point. One night in 1972 we were coming home from some party, driving down the Anzac Highway. We'd finished school and done a year at university and for various reasons neither of us had done so brilliantly that we were anxious to race back there. We were both full of the idea that after thirteen straight years of student life we were just about over it. It was late February and the air was still warm at two o'clock in the morning. There were just two weeks left before resuming for year number fourteen.

'I've got fifty dollars sitting at home,' I ventured. Fifty dollars was quite a bit of money in those days; I'd been cutting grapes at Hamilton's vineyard for three weeks solid.

'Huh,' he grinned. 'I've got fifty bucks from mowing lawns with JD.' The holiday job that became a career.

'Fuck it, let's go,' I said.

No further word needed to be said about where. Melbourne. The nearest biggest city.

His grinning face looked down at the passenger's side dashboard and his head shook from side to side as I waited for his pronouncement.

'Well, fuck it. Let's go.'

I'd three quarters expected him to say no, but maybe the voice of Kerouac was calling that night, or maybe the opening bars of 'Midnight Rambler' were still ringing in his ears.

'I'll drop you off at your joint. Grab your dosh and a couple of blankets and I'll be back in ten minutes with mine.'

We nursed private, excited thoughts and planned how we would both get into our houses and out again with supplies without waking any parents.

I did rouse my brother to tell him I was off.

'How long for?'

'Maybe a week, maybe a year.'

'Hmmm, orright,' he managed as his head rolled back onto its pillow and his eyes closed again.

*

First day in Melbourne we saw a sign outside the Flinders Street station

that said 'Workers Wanted': for loading up trains at the goods yard
down the other end of the block that was the city square of Melbourne.
So we slept in the car again and lined up at eight in the morning like
the man said. We both were hired for casual pay by the day and then
we got a couple of rooms in some house from the noticeboards at the
university. The idea was to build up some more cash from the job at the
goods and then off to Tasmania to hitch around before coming back
to load up some more train trucks and head off north for the winter.

In three days we were set with a job and a place and a plan. Except
for one thing. Along with the sign saying 'Workers Wanted' there was
another one that said 'Fireman Wanted.' Now we're not talking about
blokes who go around with funny hats and huge hoses and who win
medals for bravery every once in a while. We're talking an archaic term
that comes from guys who used to load wood up into the engines of
trains when they were fired up that way. But now it meant the job of a
driver's offsider. So if the driver has a heart attack or keels over in some
other unexpected way there's still someone there to halt the ship and
raise the alarm.

The romance of the train. Bob Dylan sang about flaggin' down the
Double E. Jimmy Rodgers was the yodelling brakeman who became
too sickly to work but even as a boy he'd taken his guitar with him
every day and remembered every story and every polyglottal song that
any tough old bastard ever growled out at smoko. Kerouac was full of
hopping freighters for that easy section of the ride to Frisco. I laughed
years later when I saw a Pee Wee Herman film where he too hops
a freighter and runs into a rustic bum; they sing raucously along to
'She'll be comin' round the mountain'. By the third song Pee Wee is
numb with boredom.

That about sums it up. Colin's job was not just a job, it was an
apprenticeship: five days a week, any time of day or night, forty-eight
weeks a year. End of travelling anywhere more exotic than Shepparton.

He did nearly the whole apprenticeship before he realised he
couldn't take it any more. It turned out to be the dullest, most repetitive

job, paralysing to both mind and digits. He told me of the freezing winds, of adjusting taps and levers with fingers deprived of sensation, of sticking the face out into the slipstream to read the signs that might be the difference between life and death.

Adventure is a matter of perception; it lives in our minds. Like pleasure, we know from experience that something is going to be pleasurable and so we may live for that thing as the one and only thing that brings our lives up from the mundane and banal. But sometimes, more often than we would like to admit, we are told that something is going to be pleasurable and so we find it indeed to be pleasurable, whether it would have been pleasurable had we been told it would be or not, if you understand my meaning.

*

'And so with the life of trains,' James agreed with me. 'We're told it will be romantic, eh, and it takes us three and a half years to realise that it's not.' He sniggered for the foolishness of our mutual friend. 'He was never going to amount to anything, though,' he went on.

The pub was beginning to fill up with the Friday-night crowd. Lawyer blokes with ruddy cheeks were tucking into red wines in glasses the size of vats. Spivvy law clerks with skinny ties drifted from the bar to the cocktail lounge and back again. The whole trial of life was in motion. I wondered about what it meant to amount to something.

'How's life for yourself, then?'

'Ah, good, good,' he said with vacant eyes. 'Work's firing along. Some of the boys'll be along in a minute.'

I got it now. When I'd bumped into him in the street, he'd been half an hour early for his piss-up with the boys from the firm. He couldn't handle hanging around that long on his own.

I drained my glass. 'So how's Lucy?'

'I told you. We broke up.' His face lost some of its rehearsed agreeableness.

'You know what I mean.'

He still looked mystified.

'Ever been told something's going to be romantic and then find out that it's just not?'

Signs of understanding appeared in his face. 'You always were a fucking smart-arse prick,' he said.

As I got up, two blokes in suits bowled in, full of anticipation, spotted us and swung straight over. James broke into smiles and there were grins and shoulder pats all round.

I had to be introduced, whether I was leaving or not.

'An old mate of mine from school,' he said. 'We just bumped into each other in the street,' he said by way of explaining my casual dress, my casual attitude, no way had he arranged to meet me. He patted me on the shoulder.

'Actually I'm just a fucking smart-arse prick,' I said.

They all laughed heartily. After all, it was Friday night and we were all good chaps.

'A standing joke, from long ago,' I heard him say as I passed through the door, not looking back.

Flinders Fields

I'd picked him up that morning in the car. His car. The one that had been sitting in the shed for the last three months while he was in low care.

'I'll miss your dad,' the nurse from Florey wing had said, as if he was never coming back.

'We've paid to keep the room on hold.'

'He just reminded me so much of my old dad. He went nine years ago.'

'It took so long to get him in here we're not letting it go.'

She busied herself with the paperwork I had to sign.

'You know he used to live up Beulah Road when he was just a lad.'

'Yep, he told us.' She smiled.

'Used to come past here on the way to school.'

'Yeeeep,' she smiled again, as if the story had been often told. Then, 'There's a lot of fluid on those lungs.'

He'd beaten the cancer five months before.

*

At the check-in, Dad smiles, grins perhaps, at the petite little girl at the desk who has to organise the whole procedure.

'Nurse has just taken someone up,' she says. We know that is code for 'It's going to take a long time.'

We sit in padded chairs either side of a little bone laminex table and face towards the gum trees and the car park and the double doors that roll open and shut with all the human traffic that comes in and out.

'Might as well leave the bloody things open,' Dad says. 'Save a lot of trouble.'

'And electricity,' I remind.

A young nurse comes past and smiles at Dad, at his hopeful, expectant face. Nurses often smiled at Dad. This one is neat, trim, pert.

'I'd be after that if I was of a marriageable age.'

'Settle down, Dad. They mightn't let you in at all if you keep on like that.'

After a silence of a few seconds in which he considered his response, 'Thought she might be good for you.'

'Hmmm, too young for me, Dad.'

He nods twice to himself, not missing the meaning. Dad was eighty-four years old.

Last time we'd been here, one of the nurses said to me that he had been the sickest person in the ward and that they'd nearly lost him a couple of times. In all his struggle he had pressed the help button less than any other person there.

*

'Hit the jackpot,' I said.

The room was flooded with sunlight. A big window spread out a view over the south-west suburbs to the high rise of Glenelg in the distance and the ribbon of sand that hit the blue sea for ten miles along the coast. Across the road and just below us were the playing fields of Flinders University; I'd played maybe two games against them thirty years or so before.

Dad came over to look. 'Uh huh,' he said, pursing his lips as if to say, 'Not bad.'

'Flinders Fields,' I said.

'Wrong war, mate,' he grinned.

*

I'd had a tough time of it that autumn. Suddenly at school I'd found myself on the wrong side of the deputy principal for reasons I couldn't fathom. Deputy principals are not people you want to be unpopular with; I soon found myself teaching in all the worst rooms, one a windowless dungeon in the centre of a dark office building. It was a depressing place where even the brightest students soon became gloomy and introverted.

When I told him I would be taking the morning off to help out Dad, he'd hitched his pants up like old blokes do when they're about to show their authority. Right there in the public waiting area, shoved his hands in his pocket and sighed, 'Jesus Christ, how long's this going to go on for?' It was the third half-day I'd had off in two months.

I didn't slap him. Not even when his eyes told me he thought I was making it all up about having this sick parent who needed transporting around from home to hospital to nursing home and back again and that there was no one else in the family who could do it.

My girlfriend had dropped me two weeks before.

I quit my job. Not because of Dad, not because of him, not because of her. I just had to get out of there.

Still, you should have seen the look on the deputy's face.

*

So I had time to do things. A long ride to Strathalbyn to see Julie seemed like the thing to do. Through suburban roads, up through the hills and their tight, hard bends, then long, golden country roads; cows and vineyards, with endless gums on either side, and a chance to flatten it and cruise head down and arse up. We went into the Victoria Hotel for lunch.

Julie and I had known each other since schooldays. Not that we went to the same school or anything. Her brother knew someone from my group and we were all in the same general neighbourhood, so we joined up to be one big gang that hung around together. Her parents were as poor as church mice but they still managed to get her into one of the Catholic girls' schools in the city.

It didn't work, though. They say that in those places the rules are so rigid that you've got to be all for it or all against it. She was all against it. Not that the parents seemed to mind that much. After all the lousy cards life had dealt them, the matter of having a daughter an atheistic dropout at the age of fifteen didn't seem even slightly unusual to them. Dad had his flagon of sherry and his telly and Mum had her ironing and her fags and they seemed not to expect or ask for anything more or less. We are but pieces of meat and the peculiar results of freakish genetic accidents anyway, or so their every movement seemed to say in its acceptance of fate and lack of demonstrable ambition.

Julie and I had a little thing for a while when we were seventeen. Just about three weeks. Once we got to being kind of adults, she'd ring up every few months and I'd pop down there to give her something to do. Give me something to do. She was with some bikie called Kenny who never seemed to do much. He was a nice enough bloke, but I still steered clear of him for some reason I couldn't quite explain.

We tucked into our lunches: chicken snitty for her and grilled fish with chips and salad for me. She looked pale, face like oatmeal and her light brown hair dropped in front of her in straggly ropes as she ate. She wore a maroon and gold hippie dress that might have been smart twenty years before, and black kung fu slippers.

'Thanks for dressing up,' I said.

Her mouth crinkled up into a smile and she rasped out of the corner of her mouth, 'Who gives a fuck?'

She looked sick. I wondered if she was taking after her old man, or her mother. Or both. Or Kenny. A fine nest of influences.

I heard from someone else that she was working on the game a few years ago, but the coppers told her to give it up after she tried to scratch some bloke's eyes out. It appears politic to develop a certain bedside manner. That whole thing is something I never asked her about. I waited for her to say something, but she never did.

'That'll put a bit of meat on ya,' I say, nodding at her schnitzel.

'I could use it.'

She is looking more emaciated every time I see her.

Two middle-aged women at the table next to us were talking loudly, about illnesses. Some women of a certain age group seem obsessed with disease, watch all the medical dramas on TV, documentaries on sickness. Amateur experts. Soon they got on to cancer. They went into a mad gale of laughter about something I didn't catch, and it took them a minute or so to return to their topic.

'It always comes back.'

'Always comes back.' Solemnly.

'Gawd rest 'em.'

'Gawd rest 'em.'

Julie doubled over her plate in mock hilarity. 'Just what you need today. Ha ha ha.'

Her exaggerated cackle did what it was intended to do. It made me smile.

'Yeah, just what I need. You finished?'

She'd stopped eating, but her plate was half full. 'Yeah, I don't eat much.'

'Waste of money taking you out.'

'You won't even get a root out of me.'

'No thanks, not with a boyfriend who looks like yours.'

She wheezed again in a role play of mirth. 'Let's get out of here,' she said. 'Place is like a fucken morgue.'

*

We walked in the river park that winds all through the centre of Strath. Rain had washed the autumn leaves into a swampy sludge at the side of the path. The falls of that morning laid about in front of us and we kicked our way through them, taking care not to slip on their glistering surfaces.

She told me about her dream. She said there was a plague of ants that were eating her alive. She said that ever since she was a kid she had been scared of ants. When they made a nest in her backyard and swarmed over the old red bricks that were the path to the lane out back, she would scream when they crawled over her feet. Her mum had to come out with the hose and squirt her clean to shut her up. But in her dream it was different. The ants were eating her alive, but it wasn't a painful or disastrous experience in any way. She was watching it all happen quite calmly, waiting for them to get down to the bone, so she could be a skeleton. As if that were some pure state she had to achieve before she would be happy, or before she could die peacefully; only then would she feel complete.

'Did they get there?' I asked.

She looked at me quizzically.

'Did they finish the job?'

'Oh, dunno. Fucken Kenny got up to go for a piss and I woke up.'

I nodded, deadpan.

'Things don't have to be as bad as people make them,' she said. 'We're all just so taught to make a drama out of everything. We are… all…so…self-important.' She spaced these words out and pronounced them so deliberately it seemed like they might have applied to someone she knew. 'What happens, happens.'

But we do have time to make something of our lives, I thought.

'Do you think we go somewhere when we die?' I asked.

'I don't know. Everyone, but everyone, wants to think they know the answer to that one. But what does it matter anyway? If we go, we go.'

*

When I went down to the country that morning, I'd felt like I was riding through a fog. It was all hard work, watching the road, shifting gears, maintaining the balance that keeps the bike working best: conscious, laboured action. But on the way back I was flying; it was not like work. The bends came and went without me even knowing they were there.

When the main road appeared, I settled into a nice cruising speed I liked and glided past anything in the way. I decided that tomorrow I would look for something physical to do. At the age of only thirty I could feel my muscles getting slack and thought about where that would go in another thirty years.

At the corner of South Road, somehow my bike seemed to be making for the right-hand lane exit to the hospital, without me really making it go there. It was a time when it seemed some greater being was guiding me.

*

Out of the lift on the fourth floor. The tightly woven beige carpet is tucked neatly up against the wall on either side. A young man in a pale blue uniform pushes an old woman in a wheelchair and I step to one side to let them pass. They both smile at me and I suppose I smile back.

Normally I go straight to the room and tap very gently on the door as I enter. I don't like talking to the nurses much. They give a professional kind of warmth. I know that yakking away to everyone is what they have to do and that it must be hard for them to keep it up all day every day, so I usually let them off the hook with me.

But this day I go straight up to the sacred zone, the nurses' station where there is a high desk on three sides and a wall at the back; where there are always three or four people and where I feel most conscious.

The girl recognises me, but I say my name anyway and who my father is. I mumble something about tests that were done and results that were due maybe today but more likely tomorrow.

'Yep, they've just come in.' She flicks through a few large envelopes which contain X-rays and the like. Eventually she stops and pulls one out and scans the one page summary that's in there with them. 'Yeeees,' she says. 'It…looks like the doctor wants to see you about something.'

'Yes, I know.'

She checks her schedule, 'But he's not here right now.'

'I already know.'

'How would you know that?'

'Not about the doctor, about my father.'

'You know…'

'Yes, I know. I've known about it since lunchtime today.'

The look on her face says that she somehow understands what I'm saying, although I don't really understand it myself.

Killing James Brown

The XP Falcon was Keith's pride and joy.

'I wouldn't normally bring it out on a job, mate, but today,' he paused momentarily for effect, 'is somethin' special.' He winked across at Brendan from behind the steering wheel.

They cruised past the place to check the side of the house for a way out if there turned out to be trouble.

'Easy,' grinned Keith. 'I'm looking forward to gettin' rid of this cunt. And you're gonna do it for us,' he grinned. 'Come on, let's get a coffee.'

Brendan's sweaty hands turned over the heavy item in his lap, tucked into its own holster. It snuggled into more expensive lining than his best Saturday-night jacket. He ripped the Velcro flap seal open and closed it again for about the fifteenth time.

'Checked your shooter, didn't you?'

'Yeah, I told you, I checked it about a hundred times.'

'Workin' all right?'

'Yeah, she's workin' all right.'

'So leave the fucken thing alone, then. You'll be giving me the willies next.'

Brendan put the gun on the floor and crossed his arms over his chest. 'Yeah, all right.'

Keith flipped the left wrist up to check the Rolex. 'Half hour up the sleeve. Let's go get a coffee.'

Keith looked across at Brendan as he pulled the car into a park. 'Look, this Nino bloke is vermin. OK? The world's better off without him in every sense.' Keith had made sure he picked up some education along the way, an autodidact was what he said, and the phrase 'in every sense' was just what Brendan had come to expect from him.

'What do you mean, "in every sense"?'

'I mean in every sense. Like, first, he is a depraved, fucking bot-rooting homo who is starting to develop a taste for little boys.'

'Yeah, all right.'

'Second, he's starting to move in on Sammi's territory.'

'You think I don't know all about that. What else?'

'Isn't that enough?'

'You said every sense. That's only two. There's got to be more than two. Otherwise it's got to be both senses.'

Keith looked across at him and grinned out of the side of his mouth. 'All right. You've got a point. But in effect two is enough.' Then after a moment's thought he added, 'All right, he's a complete deadbeat with wickedly shitful taste in every form of cultural activity. A total fucken loser.'

'I guess that covers everything then.'

'Look, mate. Your old man'd be proud of you today.'

Brendan looked down at his knees. This was the kind of situation where his hands were supposed to be shaking. But they weren't shaking, not to look at. But he had to concentrate hard to make himself stop fidgeting, to stop rubbing his hands against his thighs, scrunching them under his legs, rubbing his eyes.

'I been in this business twenty-five years, starting out about your age now.' Keith paused and held his right hand up for emphasis. 'And just look at me now,' he grinned with the lopsided glee of some crow that had been in a street fight.

Brendan looked across at a man he had known all his life. 'We getting a coffee or not?'

*

The girl behind the bar in the café yawned and didn't even look at them. Keith grins knowingly at her bored, saucy manner, one side of her mouth twisted down in a never-ending grimace. She plonked the cups down in the saucers just a little roughly, but not enough to slop any chocolate foam over the lip of the cup. She said disdain with her eyebrows. Keith liked her.

'Here y'are, nice cappuccino for brekkie,' said Keith as he put down the cups. He was tall and lean with a permanent sparkle of devilment in his eyes. To him everything was a joke that had just happened or was just about to happen. And all things were justified in his world view. 'Bitch missed out last night.' He jerked his head back to the counter and grinned again. 'Look, mate, this deadbeat is associated with the mob that bumped off your old man. And you know how I'd feel about that. Sammi thought it would be nice for you to do this job for your first time. Like a real welcome party for you; stepping into the shoes and all that.' He held out his hands in front of him and flashed his best welcome grin. Keith could do a lot of things with his hands; he could even talk with them.

'I was a trainee hairdresser yesterday.'

'Kid stuff. Fucken shit. You're better than that, boy. It's about time you started developing your potential. Fast-tracking is what they call it now. Great term that, eh?' And Keith leant back and sipped his cappuccino; he was looking forward to the morning. 'Fast-tracking.' And he shook his head in amusement. 'I'm fast-trackin' ya.'

'I just haven't had long to get used to this idea.'

'Better that way.' Keith turned serious for a moment as if this was some part of the plan that had been important. He had shaken Brendan out of bed not forty-five minutes before. 'OK, at eight o'clock the deadbeat's alarm goes off. Every morning,' and he spread his hands out again in amusement and displayed his lopsided grin, 'like clockwork.'

'That's a good one, Keith.'

'Then he goes to the shower, like virtually straight away. Within five minutes of eight o'clock every day, right? Usually takes twenty minutes in there he's so, like, up on the personal hygiene thing. I bet he poofs himself up with talcum powder, you know what I mean? Anyway, while he's fucking around in the shower we jemmy open the back door, wait for him to come out and boom. Nice and easy. Sammi don't want no bad publicity like last time, blokes being bumped off while they're watching their lads play footy on Saturday morning. That's not good. This old cock-cuddler doesn't have any kids, thank Christ, so no one'll give a shit about him.'

Keith was serious again for just one second. When Keith dropped his jocose manner you knew it was important. 'You're taking an important step today. You have to shoot him, all right. You.' He pointed his finger. 'I'm just the back-up guy. Understand?'

'You told me all this twice already.'

'The third time is the important one. The first time you tell someone something they think, yeah right, this prick's telling me something and then they forget about it. The second time you tell them they go, hey, I've heard that somewhere before and then they probably go and forget about it again. The third time you tell 'em, they think, fuck, this cunt is serious, I'd better listen to this shit. See!' Out went his hands again; it was all self-evident.

'You think I didn't listen to that stuff the first time?'

'We know you're smarter than average, boy. Way over. That's why we're...hey, fast-trackin' ya.' Out went the hands again, higher this time. It was all fitting together; Keith's universe was in harmony. 'I've got to tell Sammi you shot the prick.'

*

At eight o'clock exactly, the XP Falcon pulled up and parked in front of the house next door to Nino's. They zipped up their tops and left the hoods down. They wore jeans and runners, which for Keith was the kind of self-deprivation that proved his professionalism. He was a natty slacks-and-leather-shoes man for preference, but this morning they set off like father and son off to some Saturday morning footy match. They walked away from the house, turned down a side street and then up a little lane that went up the back of the row of houses that fronted the street where they were parked.

Keith was excited by how beautiful the set up was. 'This is so easy. Just gorgeous.'

The back gate of Nino's place wasn't even locked. Keith nudged it and shook his head in disbelief, then they crouched for a minute, listening for shower sounds. After a minute, the sudden sounds of funky soul music hit the air. Keith scowled. He had warmed up for the day at six-thirty a.m. with the final movement of Beethoven's Ninth Symphony.

'Shit. Didn't think of that,' said Keith. 'You go in to check he's in the shower. I'll stay here.'

Keith watched as Brendan crept up to the door and crouched there, listening. A full minute passed and Brendan did nothing, made no sign; he crouched with his head down, his face serious, as if in a trance, his head nodding ever so slightly in time. In frustration, Keith ran up to the back door. As he approached, the sounds became clearer: James Brown's 'Get Up Offa That Thing' bursting through the kitchen. Above that he heard the hiss of water smashing on porcelain.

'What in the fuck do you think you're doing?' Keith held his half-clenched hand in front of him and shook it for emphasis.

'James Brown. This fuckhead likes James Brown? You said he was a complete deadbeat with wickedly shitful taste in every form of cultural activity. A total fucken loser. They were your exact words, Keith.'

'Jesus, fuck.' Keith rubbed his hand through his hair. 'All right, so he's got one redeeming factor.'

'One factor? This is the soul brother. This is the man! The hardest working man in show business. Mr Butane.' He shrugged and held his own hands out, pointing his shooter at Keith as he did so.

'Keep that down. And give me the jemmy.'

Keith took the jemmy from Brendan's hand and expertly slipped it behind the lock and flicked. A brief scrunch of splintering wood and the door flapped open. He put it on the concrete outside to pick up on the way back.

Keith inspected his work. 'Like ridin' a bike, mate.' He motioned with his gun. 'In.'

Inside there was a poster of James Brown on the wall, his chest poking through a purple velour bodysuit, his cheeks beaded with sweat, wailing into a microphone pulled towards him on a stand. On the kitchen bar was a four-inch miniature statue of the man in similar pose.

'This is like a shrine,' said Brendan in awe.

Keith's eyes began to bulge. 'Shut up,' he hissed. 'Get over there,' he said, pointing to a kitchen table where there was still a mess of plates and chunks of cheese and dirty cutlery from the night before. Keith took up his position closer to the back door.

'Get up offa that thing,' came Nino's voice from the shower, 'dance until you feel better. Get up offa that thing…' On and on he went, even when the song stopped and another began.

Suddenly the shower stopped and the rustling of towel on pampered skin began. 'Try to relieve some…pressure.' Then the door opened and Nino entered the room, his hair sticking out like porcupine quills, half wet, a fluffy, white towel wrapped and tied around his lower half.

Keith and Brendan were taut, knees flexed, guns raised.

Nino sang out one last 'Get up offa …' The CD switched into 'Night Train'.

Nino looked up. 'Hey, you guys. How the fuck…' His eyes flicked over to the back door with its gaping wound then turned back to the hands holding the guns.

'Just hold it right there,' said Keith.

'Don't tell me Sammi sent you. No, this is all some terrible mistake.'

Keith glared at Brendan across the room and motioned with his gun to get on with it.

Brendan's grip on his gun began to tremble and his eyes began to moisten. 'I can't get fucken James Brown out of my fucken head. Turn that shit off, will ya.'

'Jesus Christ,' Keith rolled his eyes. 'You're kidding.'

'It's like I'm shooting him,' and Brendan nodded in the direction of the poster on the wall.

'Just fucken shoot him.'

'Turn it off.'

Keith crouched in front of the CD player. 'Fuck me dead, which fucken button is it?'

'You like James Brown?' Nino said to Brendan. 'Awesome mover.'

'Which fucken button is it?' Keith snapped, louder.

'Er, the big one on the left.'

Keith's finger jabbed at the spot and suddenly the kitchen was in silence.

'Thank Christ for that.'

'What about *Sex Machine*?' said Nino. 'You like that one? Good piano in it too.'

'Yeah, yeah, it's a beauty.'

'What the fuck is all this about? We come here to shoot the cunt, not talk about fucken music.'

There was a pause in the kitchen as Brendan's hand trembled on the trigger.

'You didn't tell me he was going to like James Brown, though.'

'I don't give a fuck if he likes fucken Mendelssohn. Shoot the prick.'

'You told me this was just some deadbeat.'

'Hey,' said Nino, his arms out appealing to Keith, 'that's not nice!'

'You didn't tell me he was gonna be a dude.'

'Yeah, hey! Now you got it!'

'It would have been all right if it hadn't been a dude that liked James Brown, for my first time.'

'Oh no, is this your first time? They should've got you someone easier.' Nino turned to Keith. 'It would have been better if you got him someone he didn't identify with for his first time. You know that.'

'Yeah, it'd be better that way,' said Brendan. 'Why don't we do someone else first? You know, some real deadbeat like you said. Then later on we could come back and do this bloke when I'm desensitised.'

'Great, now you're thinking.'

'You out of your mind, you fuckwit? We got this turd trapped like a rat.' Keith held up his fingers and counted out the advantages with his gun barrel. 'First he's got no kids, second it's Saturday morning and no one'll miss him all day, and third Sammi's gonna kill us if we don't. If you don't shoot him, I'm gonna shoot the fucken both of youse. Now shoot him.'

Brendan hesitated a moment longer. Nino grabbed at the table with the remnants of the cheese plate from the night before and picked out a large sharp knife and lunged towards Brendan. He had drawn back the knife to grab Brendan's arm when a flame flashed from Keith's gun. The blade of Nino's knife was just an inch from Brendan's guts as the flash of fire and Brendan's scream both broke the air. A shot passed through Nino's forearm, straight into his solar plexus. A small spurt of blood then Nino dropped the knife, spun round and crashed hard to his kitchen floor.

For ten seconds, silence reigned through the house. Brendan could hear proud magpies warbling outside, proclaiming their sense of place, of ownership of that house, the backyard and all the neighbourhood beyond.

Keith took four steps across the room and stood over the body. 'Well, there's your fucken James Brown mate.'

'You fucken cunt,' Brendan shouted at Nino's body.

'Can't trust anyone in this world, mate,' Keith grinned and held his left hand out in sorrowful appeal.

'You fucken cunt.' Brendan was seized with a desire to have revenge on Nino, to show him that he really had been going to kill him all along, and that he was at no time fooled by this ruse of James Brown friendship.

'Why don't you shoot him now?' said Keith, noticing the look in Brendan's eye.

'What? Now? With him dead and all?'

'Can't do any harm. Might help desensitise you, like you were saying before.'

'Fuck it. I reckon I will.'

'Yeah, that's the lad.'

Brendan took one step back and held his gun with both hands. A look of contempt stole his face as he pulled the trigger. Bang! 'You fucken…' bang! '…cunt.' Bang went the gun again.

Keith's mouth pulled back in sheer delight. 'You little beauty!' Bang! 'Two more!' Bang, bang!

Keith bent over Nino's body, seven holes now in his torso. 'That's what you call making a job of it.' Keith's face creased up in admiration. 'Never seen anything like that,' he cried, and slapped Brendan roughly on the back. 'I can tell Sammi you shot him now, six fucken times.'

But Brendan's anger had not yet subsided. He threw his gun at Nino's dead body and connected hard on the temple.

'Now, now, now, that's going too far. Have to respect the dead.'

'What'll we do with him?'

'Just leave him there. Let's go. This James Brown shit's giving me the creeps. For fuck's sake, don't get blood on your shoes.'

As Keith stepped through the back door, Brendan took one last look at the poster on the wall, the four-inch James Brown doll, the chef's knife on the floor, and the dead body beside it.

'Mate, you took an important step today,' said Keith as they walked down the lane towards the XP and patted Brendan's left shoulder with one adroit right hand. 'Sammi is going to be very pleased.'

Love the Hurt

The front room at the Tivoli had more pieces falling off it than any other place I'd seen. Torn posters of rock bands past and future looped off the wall with a sneer and showed where sheets of plaster had slipped out long before. In places the large square lino tiles had vanished from the floor and patches of beer-sodden carpet had been worn through to nothing.

The Tivoli may have been a grand place about eighty years before that time and even in my childhood it had been the home of old-time music hall, the kind of thing that is hilarious when you are an eager ten-year-old and tragic when you are a sophisticated twelve. From the outside of the Tiv there was still a glimpse of it; the façade held its dignity despite years of decay. But the veil was lifted the moment you stepped past the mahogany staircase and your feet began to stick to the floor.

On Love the Hurt night, ashen locals were clobbered out in black, black on black, and the just-out-of-bed look, at ten p.m. Like rocks in a seething ocean were some scrawny boys from out north who had settled for AC/DC T-shirts and little cloth caps; knowing they were not in their place, they exaggerated their boisterous attitude of ownership.

The walls were jammed with paper posters – The Tangerines, Five Car Pile-up, and of course Love the Hurt: all uniformly weird, I guessed. The notices are slapped on top of the last: the past is dead, and the future is never more than a week away.

Most people do not allow for smiling. There is a short bar. People crowd around each other but are too frigid to touch. Bodies held in secret spaces: together, alone. Drinkers stand as they would in an eighth-floor lift: close, but separate. There is a kind of waiting too – a sense that you are filling time up with something. That the real thing is always somewhere else, just out of reach. Next week perhaps, away, somewhere else. Melbourne.

Cassie says, 'Let's get a drink before we die.'

I love that girl. For most of the Myrtle Bank punks, two drinks a night is the limit. Not right to be seen out drunk; so much culture is grained in at convent school. But Cassie cares no fig for that.

Two lads are drinking at the end of the bar. Not sipping, drinking – guzzling almost. They wear close-fitting little leather tops made for motorbikes. One wears the cloth cap, the other a bush of curly, ginger hair. I am drawn to their pissed joviality. As I queue for drinks, I look at them, purse my lips and make to half-nod in their direction. But they see my clothes and take me for one of the others. Their conversation continues; they double in laughter at some news or reminiscence, their voices jarring through the cool.

I merge into the phalanx at the bar. When someone pushes by with their drinks you have to ease back to let them past and risk losing your space to a more assertive drinker. So we can't talk while this is happening; if I lose my place, I will be judged for it. Cassie has hung back and lit a cigarette but watches closely. I am male and I must procure. I succeed. Courage and grace under pressure. The beer is cold: we drink beer.

It's Love The Hurt we've come to see as well as to be a part of the Tiv. Cassie started telling me about them. They play Joy Division songs and all the latest Manchester stuff. Some of their own too; maybe all their own stuff now. That's why we're here, to find out what's new. But she starts to tell me more about Joy Division, as if they're the attraction, not the Hurt. She hasn't been talking about them for twenty seconds when she moves to Ian Curtis, their singer who snuffed himself rather than go to America with the band. She said they'd found him swinging in his mum's kitchen, as if that were serious validation of his credibility. I said I guessed that must have shown he didn't want to go commercial.

'He wasn't made that way,' she said with emphasis.

'But the other guys in the band were?'

'They were all excited. About going to America, that is. Not about him dying. They started a new band straight away. Sort of.'

'So if they wanted to go commercial and he didn't, then it wouldn't have worked out anyway, would it? Maybe that's what he saw. Like love gone wrong.' I gave the last three words emphasis.

She raised an eyebrow, 'Steady pardner, put down that gun.' She put her index and middle fingers to her mouth and blew the smoke away.

So I said that maybe there were a lot of other things going on in his head that no one will ever know about.

'No doubt,' she said, as if I had made such an obvious statement that I was faintly tiring her. 'People used to make fun of him because of what he wrote about. As if it was pretentious, being so dark and writing about the ugly things in life. The things that are really there. Is that the way people treat someone different? Laugh at them?'

'When they're afraid of them they sometimes do.'

'They stopped laughing. When he did it.'

'You mean they stopped laughing at you?'

Cassie's eyes were focused, but narrowed, seemingly on an object far away, out in front of us, on the other side of the room. As if she nursed in her head the seed of an idea that would bloom and ripen in its own due time. I feared her for a moment: her potential to run to extremes, her love of a dark, dead singer, and her arcane thinking, padlocked in her head.

'He might have had ideas about what's good and what's evil. But there's a lot of grey in this world. Even commercial music can be okay.'

'There is a lot of bad. Selfishness. Not much else.' She spoke like she knew.

'There's no god then? No judgement?'

Neither of us believed in this.

'No god. No judgement.'

'No good deeds.'

'All good deeds are ego.'

'No love, no ethics?'

She looked at me. 'All love is self-interest. There's nothing else.' She pulled a Peter Stuyvesant from a packet and lit it quickly. She didn't offer me one.

'If there's no ethics, Ian Curtis wouldn't have cared if they went commercial or not.'

She pursed her lips and looked up at me with a raised eyebrow as if to say, 'Not a bad try.'

'Sometimes I wish we'd never had books in the shelf at home,' I said. 'It'd be easier that way. You know I read when I was ten or so that there were so many hundreds or thousands of religions in the world. I can't remember how many it said now – in some encyclopaedia we had. Hundreds of different religions in Africa, just for starters.'

Cassie held onto my arm now, and I poked her hair behind her ears so I could see her face better.

'But I'd been to Sunday School as well, and they'd said that we were the same as people from all over the world – that we were all just as equal, so to speak. So it seemed to me that if we were telling them all their religions were wrong, and ours was right, then they weren't our equals any more. In effect we were telling all the Africans they were a mob of no-fucking-hopers.'

Cassie was thinking then, making connections for herself. 'I have a friend. He played some gospel music. You know, bluegrass, all that stuff.'

'Did he have a wispy beard?' I thought of the few bluegrass people I'd ever met. They all had wispy beards.

'Not this one,' she answered factually, as if it had been a perfectly sensible question. 'There's all this stuff about the Devil. The Devil is in nearly every song. He's always there, tempting them. As if it's a person doing it, with horns coming out of his head,' she laughed.

'Simple conceptual anthropomorphisation.'

She looked at me with eyebrows raised and lips pursed, the way she did. 'You get that,' she said.

'People think that if there's a good there always has to be an evil. If you don't have Satan, you can't have God. That's why we have the resurrection. Christ can lock horns with the Devil that way. And be perfect too.'

'Like Superman: truth, justice and the American way. Nice and clean.' She seemed to be accepting the idea that righteousness might be the way of the simpleton.

'Something to believe in is good. But grey is more real.'

'But if nothing comes from God,' she said, 'nothing means anything.'

'Maybe.'

'That means it doesn't matter if you're an artist or you go commercial.' She adopted her distant look again. 'Or if you kill yourself, or someone else.'

'Perhaps,' I tried to laugh. 'But there's a sort of conscience in us, isn't there? That's what you have to follow. And we're all different.'

'So why don't people just do things that are true to them?'

'True to them? They'd have to find out what they are first. Where is anyone going to do that? You'd have to go too far back: childhood and beyond. Do you think Love the Hurt would be wrestling with the idea of whether to go commercial or not?'

'Huh, this is commercial now. Things like this are only good before they get big. You know, when I was at school people used to laugh at me for liking them. So I dyed my hair black, even my eyebrows.'

'Black!' I couldn't see it – platinum to black, as if there was nothing in between.

'When Ian died, they stopped laughing. Did I say that already? Straight away. It was a kind of respect. He wasn't a joke any more. And it was like I had him all to myself, at least I did in that place. But now they're big. Everyone's into it. So what do you do?'

'Move on. Find something different.'

'I know I have to do something for myself.'

It was the first time she'd admitted anything. Before then she'd recited anecdotes about herself and her family, always showing her sister up in some bad light – bitchy, sluttish, superficial. But it was always controlled, like a press secretary leaking information.

We were leaning against a pillar at the back of the room waiting for the act to come on and I put my arm around her waist, under her shirt, next to her skin – a risky proprietorial gesture.

She smiled with a kind of resignation, as if I was a cute little boy who'd come in all muddy from play, and she put her hand on my shoulder, above my shirt, not on my skin. 'Try not to worry about me.'

'I'm not worried.' I lied. I cocked my head at her like an enquiring puppy.

'I'm going to do something soon,' she said. 'I know it. I can feel it coming.'

'Do something?'

'Do something, go somewhere. Don't ask me what because I don't know myself yet.' She said 'know myself' as if she might not even know who she was.

But the support act was starting and we moved up closer to the stage. The bass player lit a smoke and stuck it ostentatiously in the bridgehead so it could burn down while he played; its smoke drifted back towards him, watering his eyes. The drummer played head down, hard and heavy and almost tidy; he took his shirt off for the last song, just three minutes to make his ritual statement of freedom and individuality.

Two girls were up there with them: one very large kid sang bluesy Janis Joplin vocals and a more shapely one played guitar and did the back-up.

The large one said into her mike between songs, 'Can I have more of me on fold back, and less of Kate?'

Three pissed guys at a table in front of us picked up on it. 'Can we have less of you and more of Kate?' they shouted out sarcastic.

The large girl on stage lifted up one side of her mouth in a mock scowl, in good spirit, like she was a pro who'd heard it all before and wasn't fazed by no one.

After a while it was time for more beer and between songs I said so to Cassie. She said she didn't have much money.

She patted me on the chest and said thoughtfully, 'Most guys are too scared of me to talk about anything interesting. They just want to fuck me. I guess that makes you different.'

'Don't worry,' I replied, trying to make a joke of something that I really felt. 'I'm scared of you all right.'

She laughed, so that was all right.

'But you can't keep away, can you?' She lifted one eyebrow and smiled seductively.

I don't think I could've been more in love with her than I was at that moment. I wanted to pick her up and squeeze her to bits and take her away to some lonely spot to be together.

The crowd up front thickened, people had been drifting in for half an hour. We took our place at the edge of the serious crowd.

And Love the Hurt crept onto the stage. They all had hair that fell into their eyes, and to compound this they looked down a lot. The guy who stood at front with his guitar wore a navy blue jacket with a candy stripe of cream, and a pink scarf around his neck. The drummer had a paisley shirt of rusty gold; the bass player hid in the shadows. There was something mean about them.

The guitar sound was jangly, not crashing and annoying but insistent and lulling. The introduction was built through some picked-out chord structures and I was interested, waiting for the song to take wing fully. The chords built up slowly and then came crashing back down again and the breathless singer stepped up to the mike. The vocals followed the progression of the chords and the words were muffled in the echo of the hall and the guitars and the introverted image of the vocalist himself.

The second song came and went like the first and I began to look around me. There was a solid core of thirty or so up the front and in the thrall of the Hurt. Others propped up against the walls, arms folded, scrunching their jackets. A few were desultory at the bar, but watching anyway.

I wondered about this place. Where the patrons posed indifference but watched so closely. Where the band came dressed like pansies, but held a snarling hardness within them that was almost frightening. Where the girl I loved had thoughts I knew would never be mine. Nothing was as it seemed.

I'd finished my second beer. Cassie had closed her eyes and was swaying in time with the music, her shoulders lifting and falling, arms snaking out before her in some labyrinthine spiral dance.

'Up to scratch?' I asked.

She smiled and raised her right hand and moved her fingers up and down in a motion that resembled waves moving into the shore or the musical notes on a stave. She was saying, 'Hi, but don't bother me, I'm busy.'

After six or seven songs, I was bored and feeling claustrophobic. Then the Hurt struck up a riff that I recognised from somewhere. Obviously Cassie did too and she started nodding up and down in time with the rolling of the shoulders thing.

'Where will it end, where will it end?' the singer repeated over and over. This was emphatic, not mumbled; a climax of the confusion and dismay which has hinted its way through the repertoire, stabbing out depression over the reserved jangling of the guitars.

'This is the room, the start of it all,' and something about the 'bodies obtained, the bodies obtained, the bodies obtaaaaiiiined'. And then the 'where will it end' refrain jarred its way back to centre stage.

The song shuddered to its own inexorable end and Cassie opened her eyes and turned to me as if waking from a dream. 'That's enough.' She's satisfied now and we can leave.

As we go, she tells me what the name of Joy Division was about. A team of young Jewish women, pulled from the death camps in the

Second World War, for the use of German officers on leave. Joy not even for sale, just bodies for use. The bodies obtained, the bodies obtained.

'There's an irony in that title,' I said.

'Irony? There's only irony when there's meaning. And there's no meaning, not in anything. Weren't you listening,' she looked at me intently, then laughed, 'to yourself?'

Pearl Earrings

The stairway at the Nova was best descended carefully. Coming down from the cinema up top to the hot, dry street was steep and sudden, like cuffing a daydream with the hard truth. The steps were rude and real.

But that didn't bother Shona as she skipped down two at a time. Stumbles and falls were like prophecies; if you thought about it too much, it would happen. She stopped at the third last step, took one last feet-together hop to the street. Her short, loose dress flounced up for a moment, showing pale upper thighs that topped her thin brown legs. On her feet were new-looking blue gym boots and short lime green socks. She looked back up to Katie, who kept in touch with the handrail, connecting firmly with each step as she followed.

At the bottom, Shona perched on her left leg and did a Charleston routine with both arms swinging in rhythm with her right leg jumping forward and back, tapping the concrete blocks of the footpath with the toe of her boot.

Finally Katie joined her in the street. 'Phew,' she said, 'bit of a change down here.'

Shona held out her arms as if to embrace the heat. She stood on her toes, put her hands above her head and twirled around on the spot as people dodged her with their shopping bags and briefcases. 'It's beautiful.'

There had been a girl in the film with a huge pearl earring, the lover of the painter Vermeer. Shona knew that girl had been like her, for she too knew the secret of the sit, the pose, of interpretation; she knew something of the mysteries of art and she too held a gift for love.

Katie eyed Shona with the fear of the unknowable. They'd only known each other since Magenta DeWilde's party last year. She'd been fun that night, leading the singing and dancing; the 'life of' really.

'It's just opportunity, isn't it?' Shona blurted as if something she had in mind must have been thought by her friend as well.

'How do you mean?' Katie said soberly. This was now her stock response to Shona thinking out loud and expecting people to know her thoughts.

'I mean, that girl had a gift that the painter's wife didn't have, didn't she?'

'Mmmm.' Katie was hesitant.

'Well, a lot of people, a lot of us, would have that, wouldn't they?' Shona said, thinking of herself.

'You mean wouldn't we, don't you? Meaning you,' Katie laughed.

'I guess so,' Shona laughed too. 'But we just don't get the opportunities. I mean, who's going to come and ask us to sit, in this town?' Not having been born in Paris, or New York or London, was an inexplicable accident in Shona's life.

'You don't think you've got enough opportunities already? I mean, to do other things,' Katie checked, bringing Shona down more quickly than the steps had managed.

'I suppose. But you should be able to just…live more sensually than we do.' Shona looked around her as if the answer was there, too obvious.

In the street, people drifted carefully into bookshops and bars, pacing themselves in the sapping heat. High summer had proceeded resolutely into March and fried alive the idea that winter would ever come again; human existence had ground its way down to a matter of survival; they were waiting for the sun to go down.

'Beer time?' said Katie, changing the subject.

'Yah.' Shona wouldn't back down from a challenge like that. It was five o'clock in the afternoon and really too early for good girls to drink, but they had left good girls long behind. And after escape to the movies, escape to the pub was the only logical conclusion.

'Phew,' said Shona. Her finger had missed the black button on the traffic lights and strayed onto the broiling metal surround. It bit back at her.

'It was the pearl earrings that did it,' said Shona standing in the full sun, not seeming to notice the heat.

Katie positioned her head in the shadow of the traffic light pylon and looked quizzically at Shona. 'Did what?'

'Made her special. The girl.' Shona paused for a moment, then went on in such a low, conspiratorial voice that she was almost talking to herself. 'Some things are special, you know, items.'

'Like talismans.'

'Yah,' Shona said with delight. 'Talismans! Oh, Katie, you are so clever. They can make you strong, like you can do anything.'

'Oh, Shona.' Katie hinted doubt at the power of pearl earrings.

'Anything,' Shona repeated, and stared at the footpath.

'Come here.' Katie folded her left arm over Shona's neck.

The lights changed at last.

'How's the new man?' Katie asked as they disengaged and started up towards the Austral. She'd heard some reports and couldn't wait to dig around a little.

'Good, great. Really good, I mean,' and she brightened with pleasure at the idea of the Austral and talking about Jed, showing him off. 'Tell you when we get a beer.' And after a moment she added, 'He might even come.'

'What, here, today?' Katie was surprised.

'He might. He wasn't sure if he could.'

They bought pints of pale and sat in the street under umbrellas: hard-living girls of twenty wouldn't be seen dead with schooners these days. The canvas they sat under was decorated with images of Rasta men, dancing girls and stylised fruits of the sea. From the street you could see into the pub through the opened doors, check out the walkers and be seen by the passing traffic too – bugger the heat.

Their first gulps of beer were greedy, lustful to a fault.

'Aah,' they both exhaled. They needed that.

'So, what about it then?'

'Yah. My god, Jed Clark. What a dream. He's doing law, but his family are all medical. His mother's some sort of artist, so, interesting.'

'He didn't want to be a doctor?'

'Nah, he wanted to do something different, own man sort of thing. He's already got his first job set up, through some friend of his dad's.'

'Right. Talk about adventurous!' Katie's sarcasm went unnoticed.

'He's going to do International Law or something. I mean, he's aiming high, really high.'

'Is he nice?' Katie was more interested in what he was like than what he did.

'Oh, yah. Gorgeous, lovely.'

'How many times have you been out with him?'

'Four…or five. Something like that.' Shona knew with certainty that the total of their dates had been three. 'We went out to see his mate's punk band. At Thebarton. My god, you know, they've got this cute little pub down there, the Fleet Street or something.'

'Wheatsheaf?'

'You know it?'

'It's about the only place at Thebarton that doesn't have topless girls or Port Power posters on the walls.'

'Yah. Anyway, it was such a night. I was so pissed.'

'They have all sorts of beer down there, don't they?'

'White wine, darling. That's what did the damage. Spewed up all over their dinky little toilet.'

'My god, no!'

'You should see the thing. Little pink and purple tiles, left over from God knows when.'

'How was Jed about it?'

'He thought it was 70s retro, reckoned it was OK.'

'No, I mean about spewing up.'

'He's fine. Like I said, he's so sweet.'

'Cute too.' Katie had seen him just twice, a couple of years before, but hadn't forgotten.

'Yah, I mean, we did it on the first night. I mean, right, we're kissing goodnight and he put his hands down the back of my pants, you know, like one on each cheek. My God, I couldn't stop then. I hauled him inside and had him on the lounge room floor. Parents were out, of course. Nice thick shag pile, so he didn't get hurt at all.'

'Right,' Katie agreed with some reservation in her voice.

'Yah, sure. He'd be here now if he was coming. He said he might get held up at uni.'

'Mmmm, I guess that's possible.' Katie wasn't sure just how likely it was to be held up in Orientation Week, when students could take whole afternoons off to go to the movies. 'Did I tell you Jude's coming?' she added.

'Really…Jude! She knows Jed, I think. Through her cousin and the Wildy crowd. Right, anyway, my buy. Same again?'

'Yeah, sure. Can't wait.'

Shona gave the eye to the barman while she got the pints, but he was too busy to notice.

When she got back, Katie's neck was craned down the street. 'Jude's late, you know. Said it would only take her half an hour to ride down the river.'

'To ride, my God.' Shona thought life was too short for riding bikes.

'She says it cools her. And makes her feel good to do a bit of work on the way in. You know, earn those beers,' Katie said with an exaggerated, knowing wink.

'Perhaps she had a flat tyre.' Shona wouldn't have minded if she had. She'd only met Jude a couple of times, and briefly, a few months before, but she felt there was something cocky about her, something that didn't click between the two of them.

'She's always on time usually, or early.'

'Boring,' Shona offered, and Katie was induced to laugh along with her.

In a minute, Katie saw Jude at the lights and waved.

Jude rode up, hot but seeming happy with herself. She pulled her helmet off and shook her short black hair, flicking it up with her fingers so the sweat did not slick it down in the shape of a helmet. She wore shorts and jogging shoes and an aqua singlet which was brilliant against her tanned shoulders. Her friendly, freckled face showed white and regular teeth. 'Phew. Hi,' she said to Katie.

'Hi. You know Shona.'

'Yeah, of course, we've met, somewhere or other,' said Jude and raised her hand in salute.

Shona smiled sweetly.

'You're late,' said Katie, and tapped her watch with an exaggerated gesture.

'Oh yeah, ten big minutes,' she grinned happily. 'Sorry about that. I bumped into Jed on the way. He was with that Belinda Hastwell.' Jude delivered her news casually, but neatly, as if it had not been rehearsed at all. It had been trimmed and knocked into shape through the second half of her ride with a velvet hammer that would leave no visible bruises.

'Jed?' said Shona, more to herself than to either of them, not able to think beyond that one word for the moment.

'Yes, Jed Clark. Do you know him?' Jude asked with an upward inflection, a hint of surprise.

Shona said nothing for a moment, assessing the news, putting the situation together in her mind: Jed on the river park at five-thirty in the afternoon. But in which direction had he been heading? He could've gone home early and still be coming back in. He might arrive soon.

'Know him? Yes, of course,' she said.

'Oh, really! I didn't know that.' Jude turned to Katie. 'He was with that Belinda Hastwell,' Jude repeated herself. 'You remember her?'

'Hmmm. Vaguely.' Katie wondered whether it would be a good idea to change the subject again.

'She's doing law with Jed. Anyway, I bumped into them. I had to stop – I've known Jed since we were toddlers. Hope I'm excused.' She laughed as she finished locking her bike to the metal bolster. 'Phew, time for a beer. I think I've earned it,' she said and turned towards the bar.

Shona's eyes were unfocused, blinded by love's false security. 'Which way were they walking?' she blurted. She had to know.

'Eh?' Jude turned back, making like she had not heard the question properly.

'Into the city or out?'

'Oh, they were going out, towards St Peters. Belinda lives out there. I think they were going to her place. They have a pool, you know. I shouldn't wonder they'd use it on a night like this. Which reminds me…beer.'

She stepped quickly into the bar, light, nimble and assured. The barman flirted with her and Shona watched her smile back at him, confident and relaxed. Shona wanted to claw the freckles right off her happy little mug.

Jed was walking along the river with some law student, in the heat. He could be here drinking beer with her. Something began to rise from the pit of Shona's stomach as Jude came back with her schooner.

'My whole life just changed,' she whispered to Katie. A well of shame and hurt burst forth in a body-wracking, gasping sob. Shona leant forward with her right hand covering her eyes and cried big, wet tears onto her red face.

Katie put her arm around Shona's shoulder, produced some tissues from her bag and looked over Shona's head at Jude, who coolly sipped her beer and watched the traffic. A group of guys at the next table turned around for three seconds to look, grinned and shook their heads, then turned back to their pints.

After a minute, Jude produced a handkerchief from her back pocket and helped with the last section of the mopping up, saying calmly, 'There you go. There you go.' She didn't like to see a girl go too far down; she was the kind who took in stray cats and helped ravens with broken wings.

Shona blew her nose on a final tissue and stood up and walked in to the ladies'. When she returned her eyes were dry, and she was composed. She had spent five minutes sitting on a toilet seat staring at the coat hook on the back of the door, thinking how the purple tiles at Thebarton had made her spew.

*

Shona woke too early the next morning in her underwear and with just a single bed-sheet keeping the world away from her. She rose quickly, as she did most days, needing activity like she always did. She placed the espresso maker on the stove, always pleased by the quick movements needed to rinse the grinds from the previous time, fill it with water to just the right spot, spoon in the coffee and screw on the upper chamber.

She turned on the radio and listened to Triple J; the jangling noise and loud voices filled the room. The girl she shared with was still not back from Noosa and Shona hated the soundless emptiness. It reminded her of the half-filled houses of her childhood, places with grandparents and polished floorboards that your shoes went clumsy clunk on if you didn't concentrate on how you walked. Lengthy hallways with slowly ticking clocks and creeping drafts.

She poured a coffee and lit a cigarette. O Week was a bore but she was going anyway.

It had been a big night. The barman at the Austral had eventually flirted with her heaps. They drank two more pints of beer there and then moved down to the Exeter and had two more. Jude stayed with schooners; what an original that girl was. Then they'd gone on to the Rhino Room and started on the vodka, my god. Jude was still in her riding outfit; what a hoot. The guy on the door at the Rhino did a bit of a double take at her, but how could you keep her out? With a smile and freckles like that, you could never say no.

Jude had left early, about midnight. She'd said something unusual to

Katie that Shona wondered about now. After big nights out sometimes things came back to her in snatches. Glimpses and memories were patched back together like mosaic.

The two of them were having a conversation that was just out of Shona's earshot because of the music and the people. But just when the music died she heard Jude say to Katie, 'No, that's my limit,' or 'No, that's the limit.' She wasn't sure whether Jude had been talking about drinking or something else. Probably drinking, she decided; Jude was a bit conservative. Just after that Jude had left, giving Shona a brief hug. They'd been on the dance floor. They'd danced for hours, or at least it seemed like it.

Shona left the radio on for company. She slipped off yesterday's underwear and stepped into the shower. The hot stream on her back was from heaven and she closed her eyes and turned to place her face full into it. She could see Jude on the dance floor at the Rhino; her face had seemed to catch the flickering lights like no other face in the room. Shona had thought she was the most beautiful, perfect person she had ever seen: she was in control of everything around her. She had the natural rhythm; she had an instinct for the music.

As she dried herself, Shona remembered leaning, placing her hand on Jude's shoulder as if to tell her something. At the last moment she realised she hadn't anything she wanted to tell Jude at all, she'd just wanted to be close to the happy, healthy, freckled face. As Jude turned her head up to Shona to hear what she had to say, Shona had moved her hand to Jude's head and given her one light, dreamy kiss on the cheek. She'd made to do it again, on the lips this time, but Jude had moved her head back and stepped away, ducking through the maze of arms and legs and tiaras, back to the tables.

Shona stood in the kitchen with her towel in hand. She hoped everything was all right; she'd had a run of nights where she couldn't remember the end.

Then she was in front of the mirror. On her dressing table was a small box of jewellery. In it were a few things her gran had given her that had belonged to her mum. She picked out the pearl earrings. She remembered the film, and those long steps down to the hot street. The story of Vermeer and the servant girl who sat for him and had a gift that was timeless and indefinable. It was an instinct; it had been an affirmation of herself and the way she lived, to pack more into one short life.

But the earrings she held were not like the massive, luminous glob of lust on the girl in the picture. They were sedate: each single teardrop shape set in a modest silver housing, kept up close to the lobe, years yellowing the lustre of the jewel. She remembered the walk in the heat up to the Austral and the rasping touch of the hot metal plate at the traffic light when she had been careless with the button. It was all an affirmation somehow of how she just had to be.

The rest of it came back to her now. She couldn't wipe the bad parts away this time: the arrival of Jude – her news. Sitting in the toilet, staring at the door. She'd blamed the purple tiles at Thebarton. She sat on the edge of the bed and held her head in her hands. The tears that filled her eyes this time came from somewhere deeper. She wasn't sitting on view in Rundle Street, but naked on the edge of her bed at home alone.

She clasped the pearl earrings to her chest and felt their power. In the thickening feeling around her eyes and in her temples she saw a shadow, a figure dressed in white, a wedding dress, not much more than thirty. Like her, but not her, her mother stepped out of the wedding picture in her dressing table and gazed evenly across nineteen years of time. Shona's soul contacted that part of life where live the vast hordes of the dead. In her mind, Shona put the pearl earrings in the figure's ears; her hands placed them in her own ears. She was protected now, by the earrings, by her mother. The ordinary world was left behind.

Shona stood up and looked at herself in the mirror, naked save the single, silver-clasped jewel on each side of her head. She walked the long passageway soundlessly, her bare feet gliding over the hallway runner. She walked with her mother; she was her mother.

Her hand lightly touched a silver button on the machine in her kitchen; the jarring noise of Triple J was cut dead magically. She walked through beautiful silence, on the welcome cool of kitchen tiles, and pushed aside the full-length glass of her back door. On the grass of her tiny back lawn she stood up on her toes; she raised her hands above her head and twirled around, drenching in the warm morning sun like some ancient Druid or Aztec, opening and transforming.

Snake

'Poppy, love, is he going to just go like the others?'

'Perhaps I just love him. Doesn't that mean anything.'

'Poppy,' she laughed, 'you are such a tonic. Such a pretty girl, still. You're the envy of everyone with that figure. I'm sure men still want to use you.'

Poppy Larkin pushed her shoulder-length honey-blonde hair behind her ears and said nothing.

'Didn't you say yourself that he came home late the other night, in a ramshackle state?'

Poppy didn't know why she had to be the only one who couldn't have a partner who came home late in a ramshackle state from time to time. 'I do that sometimes too,' she said. 'Don't you?

'You said yourself he was drunk, ruffled hair. Lipstick on the cheek. What else do you need to know?'

'It was only on the cheek. A farewell for some woman off to Canberra. I only told you about it because he looked so funny,' she said with regret. 'You don't think…'

'I don't have to think.'

They were at the Universal. A bit unusual, Poppy thought, to come here. Regina had to drive in, and park in a station, and then drive out again at the end. Poppy only had to walk across the park from Kent Town, so the whole thing suited her and not Reg; that's the part that was so unusual.

'A bit of shopping in the town,' Regina had said. Poppy had never known her to shop anywhere but Burnside; she had even proselytised the matter. 'It's all here, and better quality. Why would anyone want to go into that dreadful Mall?' People came from all over to go to the Mall. And to Rundle Street. That was the problem. The Mall in particular was too close to the train station that brought them in from the far north and the deep south. 'They have their own Westfield things out there. Surely that should be enough for them,' Reg had said to her once, years before.

The Universal was so noisy that sometimes it was like a whole social movement that swept you in with it. But this time every clank of bentwood chair against hard tiles smacked her in the ear, and the honking ha-has from neighbouring tables made her think of Patsy from *Absolutely Fabulous*, made her shudder. And he might walk past any minute; this was his street.

Reggie was not distracted by anything, but lifted her voice without thinking to join the tympany – another breaking glass in the cut-crystal crowd of voices. 'Of course this place is the jewel,' she sang out, fluting above the din and with a sigh to the rest of the street. 'You've not heard of the chef? The next Cheong.'

Poppy poked at her noodles and thought that it was not far off what she could make for herself at home. 'What's he good at?'

'Everything. But all these failures hanging about here,' she waved her hand at the world outside, 'endlessly walking up and down and pretending to be doing something.'

'Doing something?'

'Doing nothing in reality. All pretending to be artists and having breakfast at half past ten in the morning.'

Eoghan had breakfast around here sometimes, around half past ten in the morning. Poppy was silent.

'What have you been doing anyway? In the last few weeks?' Reg changed the pace. Poppy was such a dear, but a trouble to herself if not looked after. Past fifty and still getting about in op-shop clothes. Never really settled down to anyone at all, and now this boho with a weird Irish name.

'He has an exhibition coming up at Zounds. It'll put him right back on his feet.'

Reggie held Poppy's hand for a moment before returning to her squid tentacles. She smiled sadly. 'Always in the offing, aren't they, exhibitions? About six months away?'

Poppy looked down at her noodles, but lifted her still pretty head and spoke up boldly. "That's about what he said as a matter of fact.'

Reggie raised her eyebrows as if in astonishment. 'An exhibition can be six months off for quite a few years, you know.'

Even Poppy put her hand to her mouth and tittered. 'I know.' She didn't care terribly whether his exhibition went ahead or not.

'Everyone's so concerned. We can't just let you…disappear on us.' To Reggie, all her friends from the old school years had to be somewhere within a manageable arm's reach.

Poppy thought about 'everyone' for a moment. 'If I ever disappear, it will be because I want to disappear,' she said. She stretched her hands out in front of her face, as if she were Circe holding up a libation bowl to some pagan god, or trickling poison into an enchanted pool. Then she rasped out, in a hoarse whisper, her eyes bulging like a gypsy fortune teller in long gone carnival days, 'Disappear.'

'Poppy, love. I know you won't disappear.' Reggie brought Poppy's hands down from in front of her, folded them together on the terra firma of the polished wood table and patted them three times. 'We'll all be fine.'

'He's quite lovely sometimes, you know. When I'm with him and he's like that, I feel like I just don't have to worry about anything, ever again. I feel like I don't have to think about what I say, I can do just what I want to do. It's so natural. Everything just flows.'

'I have met him, you know. He does have a sort of perverse charm about him.'

'He's taught me a few things,' Poppy said innocently.

Reggie raised one eyebrow. 'Well, let's not go into that!'

They laughed together like they did when they were schoolgirls. Poppy blushed and put her hand up to her mouth as if to stifle her titters and then collapsed over her bowl of noodles.

'What kind of things?'

And they laughed again.

'Don't be indiscreet, darling. You can't be telling your secrets all over town: things get around.' Was Reggie warning her about other people, or about herself? 'It'll come back to hurt you when this is all over.'

When this is all over. What was the meaning of over? And why shouldn't things be over when they really were over? Reggie's marriage was still going, intact as far as the public eye was concerned, twenty-five years after it was really over. Why couldn't you just live? Without it.

She saw herself in six months' time, if she talked about the exhibition and it never happened. If she talked about all the things they did together and then Eoghan gave her up for another girl. It might be embarrassing. But if you didn't live for love, what did you live for?

'I'm starting not to care what gets around.'

'He is having an influence, isn't he?'

'Reggie, he's got stuff up all over the place.'

'You mean he's made stuff-ups all over the place.'

'Oh, Reggie.'

'One rusty bit of tin stuck up in some obscure corner of the Mt Lofty Botanic Gardens.'

'It's right out the front.'

'1982.'

'Well…'

'When he was going out with Prunella Wishart. He threw the leg over and she gave him a leg up. They'd move something decent in there if they had any funding.'

'I know,' Poppy sighed. 'They would, wouldn't they?' She knew it. She knew it wasn't much of a piece and they'd got it cheap and it was supposed to be the start of something big for Eoghan: the CV entry that opened doors.

'Has he thought of anything new in twenty-eight years?'

'Not really.' She smiled.

They laughed. They laughed out loud. They connected like the friends they had been for thirty-five years. And suddenly she looked around and laughed inside herself at the other diners; they were clanking cutlery and making noise, braying endlessly at each other, but it was all so contrived, a comedy really.

'Still going around in circles, of sorts. The latest one is called *Moonscape*.'

'Don't tell me: half moons all welded up in a pattern?'

'Some full, some half.'

'Cosmic!'

The third glass of sauvignon blanc was having its effect.

'Poppy, darling, you must beware. Relationships can go on too long when the sex is brilliant.'

'How would you know? You've been with Phillip for nearly thirty years.'

Reggie raised one eyebrow.

'How can you keep having sex with the same dentist for that long? Even if he is a specialist.'

'With big ears.'

The tears came to their eyes.

'You can't hold on to those.'

'Be careful, Reggie. You can't be telling your secrets all over town.'

'There's more angles to the marriage thing than you might think, Poppy: enough on that subject. Anyway, love, it has been such a hoot to catch up. You must come to the school reunion in three weeks.'

'Lord,' thought Poppy, 'the school reunion.' It had been a few years since she'd dropped out of all that. She was caught by waves of revulsion and fear, and then the odd memory of fun they'd had in the far past. Some of them weren't too bad. For a moment she weakened.

'I'll book you in with Winnie. Oh, you will be such a piece.'

'A piece?' said Poppy.

'A piece of good news for everyone. They're dying to see you.'

And the entry was made in Reggie's diary with a flourish.

*

She was the last to arrive. Ten or twelve of the girls at a long table, probably eleven, she thought, one short of a proper jury. She was to make the twelfth. Of course, an even number, a dozen, at a squared off and properly set up table. It didn't look so much of a formal reunion as a boisterous gossip club in its habitual haunt: the monthly catch-up. Some looked as if they'd come from gym, or tennis; some from the dress shops on the Parade. She with her hair down, vermilion shirt under a shift dress of very fine black and white checks, zipped at the back with tan suede boots. She looked as if she'd tried too hard and not got it right.

The assortment of grins and smirks told her she had been talked about in the last five minutes.

'Poppy, how wonderful you look.'

'Such an interesting outfit.'

'We've been hearing all about you.'

'Do come and sit here.'

'Tell us all about it.'

'What tricks have you learnt this week?'

Tricks? Were they laughing with her or at her? It was just a chat over lunch. She'd said a few things about what she did with Eoghan, as girls do. But Reggie had told her things about her tennis coach that made her gasp. Her tennis coach, wasn't that the total cliché? Perhaps gym instructor was the ultimate.

Poppy looked around to find Reggie but she was already up at the bar arranging something with the restaurant, picking up a bottle of savvy. She came back to her place at the other end of the table; she didn't turn around.

Poppy heard the voices around her and said nothing. She studied her table setting and listened. The crowd of voices had forgotten her already. Someone she thought may have been called Phoebe something began talking about her temperamental vineyard in the Clare Valley, as if it were a person, her dear little vineyard, how it had taken her family years to establish properly. It seemed the more love you ploughed into a project, the more it gave back, although there was just no telling about the weather. A quick turn in the discussion followed, about how cold the winter was, as suddenly no one seemed very interested in Phoebe's vineyard.

Poppy stood up in her place. Her left thigh brushed the table and its legs scraped loudly against the pinewood floor; half-full wine glasses jostled about and hands shot out to save them from a fall. A pause in chatter. Faces looked up the way they do when a fork is tapped on a wine glass to call attention to an after dinner speaker. Their eyes bored holes in Poppy Larkin's body and picked like crows at what was left of her inside. It was some turning point in her life, or at least a turning back gone wrong but easily enough righted – a what-was-I-thinking moment. The handle of her bag was in her hand, it had never left her lap; she shook her head and turned for the ladies'. The faces were not in front of her now, just the stage-whispered final words behind her back, 'Still sensitive.'

From the toilet there was a small corridor to the parking lot at the back of the restaurant; Poppy slipped out there. No chance of meeting anyone coming in there, as she had been the last to arrive. She might be watched from the window, but better that than going past the lot of them again. To get back to Kent Town she had to walk all the way up the block to William Street and back again up Osmond Terrace. She would disappear; into the arms of her man at best. To Cambodia, India, Morocco, anywhere. Anywhere but here.

She thought of what she had told Reggie about her and Eoghan, about the kind of things they shared with each other: authentic, intimate things – life reduced to gossip that went the circle within a couple of days. They would talk about what they did with their husbands. Or with someone from the tennis club. Or their tennis coach, or life skills coordinator, or personal trainer. And they'd talk about her as if she had just joined the Communist Party. Their talk would turn from polite to perverse and back again and inside out and around in circles and never seem to amount to much.

But now she knew what she wanted, and how she wanted it. It would somehow repudiate them, slap them in their faces. She stepped forward with more purpose now. Down the Parade, downwards toward the city, past the oval, Norwood v Port this Friday night, past the gallery where his sculptures will one day stand, past the Old Colonist, past the intersection of five roads where she walked against the red light in the bright afternoon sun. Past the college on the left; leave that all behind. As far as Kent Town and home.

He had been different these last two weeks. Remote. But she blamed herself for that now. She had been thinking about lunching, going back to that old gang. She had talked about it, too much. Like she did sometimes but couldn't stop. Out of nervousness perhaps. It had put a gulf between them. How foolish she had been to be sidetracked, by Reggie. She knew better now.

It was even exhilarating to be leaving something at last, irrevocably; the relief of shedding skin, like a snake from hibernation into the springtime sun. The spirit entered her as she walked in that sun and she became that snake. She felt as free now as at any time in her life. If he was there he was there. If he was not she would wait. She would leave. She would return. It did not matter.

She turned her key in the lock. The sound was different. Raw, jangle. Not the confident plangency of male part into female. Her step on carpeted runner. Even that. Puss came to greet her. She looked up to mummy with a worried face, a plaintive meow. House felt like an open inspection.

His books were gone from the shelves in the study, bottles from the rack. Wardrobe empty. All his meagre clobber taken, and all her own things perfectly in place. Dishes washed and neatly stacked for her to put away: the usual routine. Stainless steel top screwed onto coffee jar and put away in place. He'd finally learnt where everything went, she smiled. Somehow that felt like something.

A note was on the kitchen table: 'Gone to Tassie. See you when I get back?' And there was his name underneath: Eoghan. Not signed, more printed. And then below that some more words, 'Wasn't really working out, was it.' No question mark: a statement.

She sat in the nearest chair as if to let it wash her, soak her. But in a moment she was on her feet, through the house to the front door and out into the street, as if his mate's utility would be just disappearing into Dequetteville Terrace and she would grasp one final glimpse of him.

A desultory vehicle sauntered past, then another, going the other way. A lazy afternoon surrounded her; peak hour not yet begun. Steady April sun through the trees played patterns on the path. She turned around to look at her empty house, puss licking paws in open doorway. The sun felt warm on her neck. She retraced her steps to the door and the puss followed her inside.

The Beach

'Well, when I was twelve, something happened that made me look at the world differently.' I started in a lecturing style which I found comfortable because it afforded an arm's length irony that I didn't really feel. 'Looking back, I'd say it was the day I began to distrust the world, if you think that's an important change.'

'Poor baby.' Cassie was not buying any adoption of distance.

'Still, you could say that nothing happened at all. Just two people sitting on the beach and a soft breeze blowing in: the gentle sou'wester that brings relief at the end of a hot day.' Wistfully.

'If you'd get on with it, then I'd know,' she said, pulling out a nail file to give a physical dimension to her own assumed distraction.

'It was hot. Father was with us so it must have been a weekend or Australia Day or sometime between Christmas Eve and about the twelfth of January when they all go back to work. Not enough people buy insurance around New Year.'

'She's a fluky game all right, your insurance.' Cassie shook her head sadly.

'I think I'd been bad, naughty…annoying, something like that.'

'Perhaps you were being punished for not getting on with some story.'

'I was isolated from the rest of the family, outside the umbrella. We had one of those shades scissored on to a wooden pole that twisted into the sand on a metal point. I was making sandcastles – that's what makes me think I must have been playing up. If I'd been told by my mother that I was being childish or foolish or something, I'd have headed straight into the sun to make sandcastles, just to show how juvenile I could really be. Anyway. I was showing them how much I just really didn't need them all. And of course my mother countered by arranging a sortie to the ice cream shop at that very time. "I think Eoghan is too deeply involved with his moats to be interested."'

'I remember Mum said, "His father will watch over him," as she led the ice creamers away. I watched them pull away to the shop, not a backward glance for me from one of them, so no point in making castles any more. My father was in his canvas-covered chair, asleep in the shade, his straw hat pushed forward over his eyes, his left arm pinning the newspaper on his lap. Nothing moved. Outside our shelter there was all the usual buzz of movement: families at cricket, lovers on rugs with radios, kids with dogs and Frisbees. You know, regular holiday life. But nothing about my father stirred. It was as if he was dead.'

'Was he?' At least she was listening.

'My first thought was that I could've swiped some money from the pants lying there on the rug and run away to the other shop, the opposite direction from the one the rest of the family went to, and scored my own ice cream. I could have raced down there and raced back so I would be there with my ice cream when they all returned: a triumph. On the other hand I could've stayed away just long enough so my mother and her ice cream party would get back first and find me gone. My old man would be in the shit, asleep on the job, and me no doubt abducted and buried under a slab of concrete somewhere in Somerton Park, you know, the next Beaumont kiddie.'

'Now that's somewhere you don't want to go.' Cassie wagged her finger in appreciation of this sentiment.

'You know, our mothers used to tell us that if a strange man stopped us in the street and offered chocolate, then on no account were we to go with him. This was what we would nowadays call a mantra. We used to joke that, obviously, no way would you go with the man, but if he was offering Caramello, then maybe, just maybe, it might be worth it.'

'Hilarious.'

'Anyway, my father was a big, fit bloke, or so I thought. A dominator. But here on the beach, asleep, with his right arm flopped down on the side of the fold-up chair, he looked more vulnerable than I'd ever seen him. His bathing trunks were tight up under his belly and his posture was crunched up in the chair so a roll of fat looped over the edge of the bathers. A life of chops and lunchtime beer and patting backs was poking out there, no mistake. He was getting older.

'I crept up closer. His legs were still wet from wading and particles of sand hung on to them, like sugar onto a pair of buttered knives. I inspected his toenails at close range, which is something you don't normally get to do. Usually you just see them flashing in and out of socks every once in a blue moon. The toenails were starting to get yellow and you could see the tinea he was always moaning about. But now it wasn't just a word, it was really shitty red blotches. The newspaper lay over his crotch with the back page already read and hanging by his side. Even though he was dozing, his thighs and knees stayed together to keep the rest of it there in place. It made him look silly.

'I went up closer still. I reckon I would have looked more like an inquisitive dog, on all fours, with its snout stretched and sniffing. I could see the hairs on his nostrils wafting faintly in the breeze, my face no more than a foot from his ear.

'My father was the enforcer, the man with the strap, the big bloke who showed me how to kick a football through a goal with the wrong foot. That day he looked like a big baby.

'Just at that moment the loose page of the newspaper flapped up in the first stirring of the afternoon wind, the proverbial sea breeze.

'He snorted awake, pushed his hat back and, sort of dazed and unfocused, he looked at me vaguely. "What are you doing?" he said, not angry, but surprised, and he looked around like he didn't know what was going on.

'I spoke my first truly cheeky words to him. "You were asleep. Should've been watching over me."

'Father frowned.

'"Anything could happen out there," I said, using my mother's words and waving towards the castle and the beach and everything else. "You can't forget what happened to the Beaumont kiddies." I stretched it even further.

'"Hmmrgh," was all he could manage.

'No belting, no threats – no mother present, no urger. When it came to the crunch, and this was the crunch, he couldn't give a stuff about all those discipline things he'd been made to do. I began to wonder how many times I'd been alone with my father before, without even my brother around. It occurred to me that this might even be the very first.'

'So he was a man of straw.'

A man of straw could go up in flames. He'd endured the war and made it in business; he wasn't like that.

'Sand,' I said after a moment's reflection. A wave of purpose could eat at his foundation; he was going with the current like anybody else.

'I thought this wasn't going to be a story about mirages.'

'I guess it was in a way.'

'They're all different to what they make you think they are,' she said.

'Who are?'

'People. Grown-ups. Nothing is as it seems.'

'Well. We're grown-ups now.'

'Yes, of course.' She smiled sadly. 'I nearly forgot.'

'But I learnt something from that – about the bluff. Some people intimidate. But it's the position that does it, not the person. Or it can be. I've known it since that day.'

'Okay, so what did you do about it?'

'There was a period where I stood up to my father, to both of them. I got the strap a lot. My big brother watched the whole thing as if it was a huge joke.'

'The troublesome second child, eh.'

'And it was just that, a joke. The dog was my best mate.'

'I knew that dog would come into it somewhere.'

'She'd come into my room and put her face on my knees and I'd talk to her.'

Cassie made whimpering sounds and an exaggerated sorrowful face.

'When I married Rosemary pretty early they thought it was the end of the fight. They'd won.'

'Why did you get married then?'

I scratched around a moment for an answer, but had to tell the truth. 'I guess I was sort of in love. In a puppy dog way, of course.'

'There's that dog again.' Cassie shook her head.

'And everybody expected it. I suppose that's all I can say.'

'Some rebel.'

And it was true; I had gone along with it. How did the rebel get pulled back into the fold? I could have jumped into an FC Holden and just driven away and never come back. What had made me wait so long? Why had I gotten so deep before I blew up? I felt as if some image I'd created for myself had melted away like that sandcastle at high tide.

And I learnt then that character was destiny, or that it would be for me from that moment. And that I was not my father, and that he was not his father. And I saw something of impermanence and the priceless nature of life. And I saw before me, stretching out for endless years, the story of an individual who would not become corrupted, who would do things his own way. I saw before me the ultimate delusion.

'Interesting story. I mean, truly…interesting,' she said as if that might have been a surprise to her.

I thought for a moment that perhaps I had become more interesting to her. Looking back, I think it may have been the moment I lost her forever.

www.ingramcontent.com/pod-product-compliance
Lightning Source LLC
Chambersburg PA
CBHW020346110726
47898CB00003B/1065